For Meredith, a fellow grand van fan. —K. N.

To my dad, David W. Digby, PhD, with thanks for all
the mind-expanding hippie van trips. —C. C.

STERLING CHILDREN'S BOOKS
New York

An Imprint of Sterling Publishing
1166 Avenue of the Americas
New York, NY 10036

Text © 2015 by Kim Norman
Illustrations © 2015 by Carolyn Digby Conahan
The artwork was created using watercolor paints on paper.
Designed by Andrea Miller, Amy Trombat, and Philip Buchanan

ISBN 978-1-4549-1063-3

Distributed in Canada by Sterling Publishing
c/o Canadian Manda Group, 664 Annette Street
Toronto, Ontario, Canada M6S 2C8
Distributed in the United Kingdom by GMC Distribution Services
Castle Place, 166 High Street, Lewes, East Sussex, England BN7 1XU
Distributed in Australia by Capricorn Link (Australia) Pty. Ltd.
P.O. Box 704, Windsor, NSW 2756, Australia

For information about custom editions, special sales,
and premium and corporate purchases, please contact Sterling Special Sales
at 800-805-5489 or specialsales@sterlingpublishing.com.

Manufactured in China
Lot #:
2 4 6 8 10 9 7 5 3 1
05/15

www.sterlingpublishing.com/kids

This Old Van

by KIM NORMAN

illustrated by CAROLYN CONAHAN

STERLING CHILDREN'S BOOKS
New York

This old van, she passed ONE,
shining in the rising sun.

With a click clack rattle rack,
ready for some fun,
this old van says,
"GOOD-BYE, ONE!"

This old van, she passed TWO,
friendly flaggers wave her through.

With a click clack rattle rack,
tooting at the crew,
this old van says,
"GOOD-BYE, TWO!"

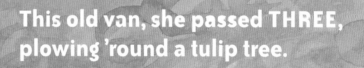

This old van, she passed THREE,
plowing 'round a tulip tree.

With a click clack rattle rack,
baggage flying free,
this old van says,
"GOOD-BYE, THREE!"

This old van, she passed FOUR,
roaring toward the grocery store.

**With a click clack rattle rack,
pedal to the floor,
this old van says,
"GOOD-BYE, FOUR!"**

This old van, she passed FIVE,
zigging up a zaggy drive.

Fletcher County Park

Vintage Car
Parade Today

ROCK IT

With a click clack rattle rack,
when will she arrive?
This old van says,
"GOOD-BYE, FIVE!"

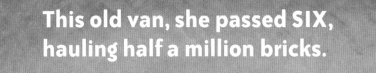

This old van, she passed SIX,
hauling half a million bricks.

With a click clack rattle rack,
spitting oily slicks,
this old van says,
"GOOD-BYE, SIX!"

This old van, she passed SEVEN,
honking horns at Hot Fudge Heaven.

With a click clack rattle rack,
flat on Route Eleven,
this old van says,
"GOOD-BYE, SEVEN!"

Route
11

This old van, she passed EIGHT,
riding high as shiny freight.

With a click clack rattle rack,
now she's running late,
this old van says,
"GOOD-BYE, EIGHT!"

This old van, she passed NINE,
just before the county line.

All-State Youth Championships Today!

Groovytown Schools

welcome to Vroom! county

Boot

Go, Scooters!

...Schools

With a click clack rattle rack,
glad to see the sign,
this old van says,
"GOOD-BYE, NINE!"

This old van, she passed TEN,
dodging dirt clods now and then.

With a click clack rattle rack,
wipers on again,
this old van says,
"GOOD-BYE, TEN!"

This old van, caked in grime,
picks up speed for one last climb.

With a click clack rattle rack,
proudly in her prime,
this . . . old . . . van . . . is . . .

All-S
Do

ST

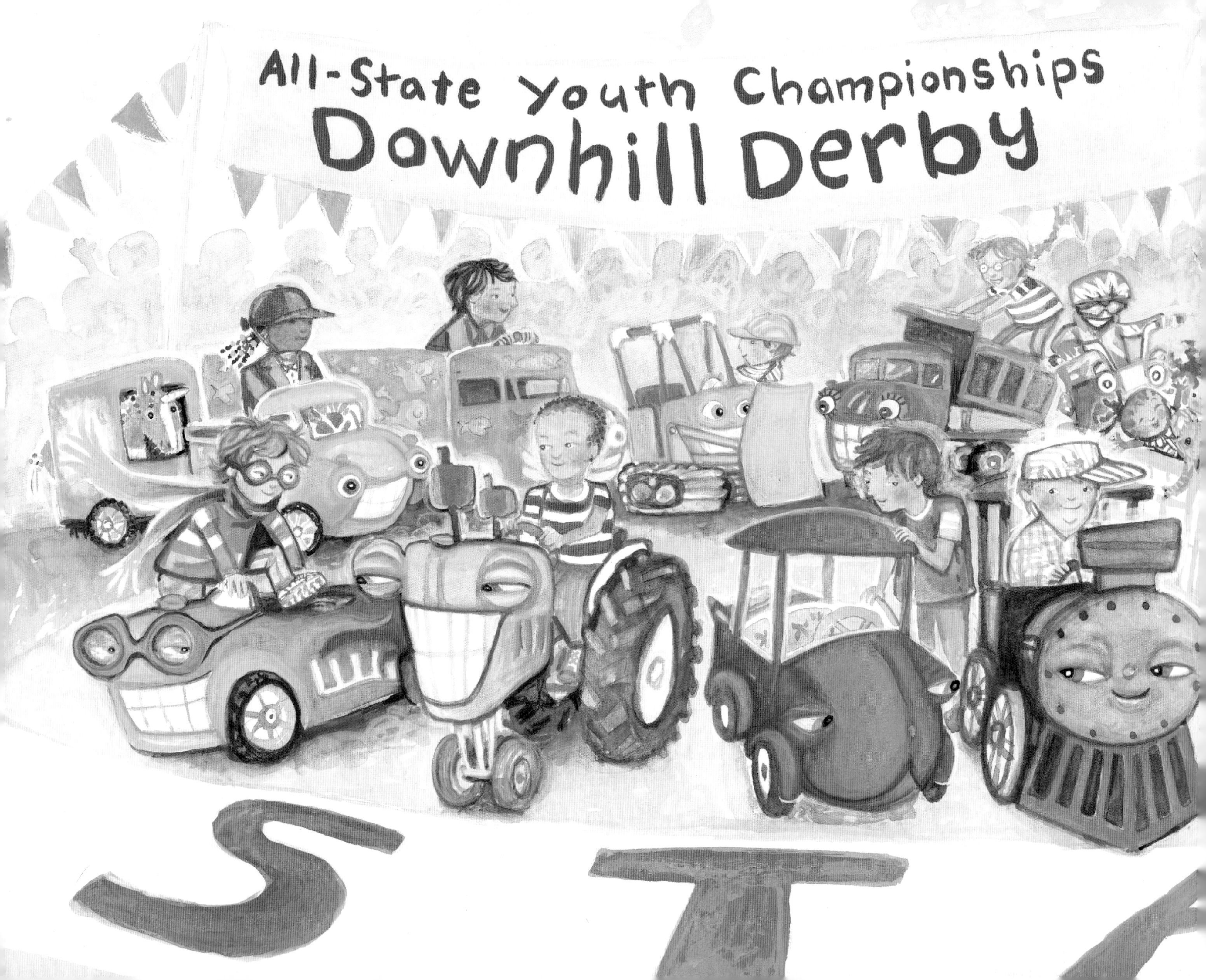
All-State Youth Championships
Downhill Derby

Just in Time!